# The Tortoise and the Scare

# Nancy Drew

## *CLUE BOOK*

#11

# The Tortoise and the Scare

BY CAROLYN KEENE * ILLUSTRATED BY PETER FRANCIS

## Aladdin

NEW YORK   LONDON   TORONTO   SYDNEY   NEW DELHI

# ALADDIN

An imprint of Simon & Schuster Children's Publishing Division
1230 Avenue of the Americas, New York, New York 10020
First Aladdin paperback edition March 2019
Text copyright © 2019 by Simon & Schuster, Inc.
Illustrations copyright © 2019 by Peter Francis
Also available in an Aladdin hardcover edition.
NANCY DREW, NANCY DREW CLUE BOOK,
and colophons are registered trademarks of Simon & Schuster, Inc.
All rights reserved, including the right of reproduction in whole or in part in any form.
ALADDIN and related logo are registered trademarks of Simon & Schuster, Inc.
For information about special discounts for bulk purchases, please contact Simon & Schuster
Special Sales at 1-866-506-1949 or business@simonandschuster.com.
The Simon & Schuster Speakers Bureau can bring authors to your live event.
For more information or to book an event contact the Simon & Schuster Speakers Bureau
at 1-866-248-3049 or visit our website at www.simonspeakers.com.
Series designed by Karina Granda
Book designed by Heather Palisi
The illustrations for this book were rendered digitally.
The text of this book was set in Adobe Garamond Pro.
Manufactured in the United States of America 0219 OFF
2 4 6 8 10 9 7 5 3 1
The Library of Congress has cataloged the hardcover edition as follows:
Names: Keene, Carolyn, author. | Francis, Peter, 1973– illustrator.
Title: The tortoise and the scare / by Carolyn Keene ; illustrated by Peter Francis.
Description: First Aladdin hardcover/paperback edition. | New York : Aladdin, 2019. |
Series: Nancy Drew clue book ; 11 | Summary: Nancy, Bess, and George are excited about
their school trip to the wildlife refuge, but when they arrive, the animal
Nancy most wants to see, a sixty-year-old tortoise, is on the loose.
Identifiers: LCCN 2018023376 (print) | LCCN 2018029099 (eBook) |
ISBN 9781534414846 (eBook) | ISBN 9781534414822 (pbk) | ISBN 9781534414839 (hc)
Subjects: | CYAC: Wildlife refuges—Fiction. | School field trips—Fiction. | Turtles—Fiction. | Mystery
and detective stories. | BISAC: JUVENILE FICTION / Mysteries & Detective Stories. | JUVENILE
FICTION / Social Issues / Friendship. | JUVENILE FICTION / Readers / Chapter Books.
Classification: LCC PZ7.K23 (eBook) | LCC PZ7.K23 Tor 2019 (print) | DDC [Fic]—dc23
LC record available at https://lccn.loc.gov/2018023376

# ✻ CONTENTS ✻

# Chapter

## GUESS WHO?

Nancy Drew stood in front of her science class with an index card in her hand. Her best friends, George Fayne and Bess Marvin, were sitting in the back row. She stared down at the card, wanting to give everyone a clue that was good, but not too good. She didn't want them to guess the answer right away.

"I'm tiny . . . ," she said. "And I have spines and short legs."

"Hmmm . . . ," Mrs. Pak, their teacher,

murmured. She glanced around the classroom. "What could she be? Does anyone have any ideas?"

Jamal Jones's hand shot up in the air. He always got straight As and had guessed the last two correct answers. Nancy held her breath, wondering if he'd get it right.

"Are you a porcupine?" he asked.

"You're so close!" Nancy gave another clue, and she was sure he'd get it right this time. "I can roll up into a ball if I'm scared. . . ."

"Oh! You're a hedgehog!" Jamal cried.

"Very good!" Mrs. Pak said, taking the card from Nancy. It had HEDGEHOG written on it in block letters. "This class is going to be so prepared for our field trip tomorrow. I'm sure all the guides at the River Heights Wildlife Center will be impressed."

Nancy took her seat next to her friends. Bess's long blond hair was pulled back in a ponytail as she leaned over her book. *The World's Most Exotic Animals* was open to the page about servals. The spotted cat looked like a cheetah with bunny ears.

"Their ears are so cute," Bess said, pointing to the pictures. "They're so much bigger than their heads! I hope we get to see one tomorrow."

"I want to see a ball python," George said.

"Those are terrifying!" Bess whispered.

George and Bess were cousins, but they couldn't have been more different. George had short brown hair and brown eyes, was athletic, and was not easily scared. Bess always feared the worst would happen, and Nancy had only ever seen her play sports in gym class. Together the three of them made up the Clue Crew. They worked together solving mysteries around River Heights. They'd even recovered a telescope that had been stolen from a local museum.

Harry and Liam McCormick went to the front of the class. They were identical twins, with orange hair and freckles, and they liked doing presentations together whenever Mrs. Pak would let them. They'd just moved to River Heights in September, and were obsessed with Antonio Elefano, the biggest prankster in Nancy's grade.

The twins were constantly doing things to try to impress him. Just the week before they'd climbed thirty feet up a tree trying to get his attention.

"Ummm . . . we're red," Liam said, staring at his card. "I mean I'm red."

"And we have giant wings!" Harry added.

Nancy thought they might be parrots . . . maybe sun conures, but that seemed too obvious. They'd been studying so many exotic animals that she sometimes got them mixed up. Was it possible they were scarlet macaws?

"I don't think we are red . . . ," Harry said quietly to his brother. "Aren't we blue?"

Mrs. Pak leaned over their shoulders to get a better view of their cards. "I think you're red and blue. And maybe a few other colors too."

"We're very colorful," Liam agreed.

George raised her hand. "You're a scarlet macaw."

"That's right! She's right," Liam said. He seemed excited that someone had guessed the correct answer, even though they were a bit

confused about which bird the macaw was.

Mrs. Pak moved on to the next lesson, pulling up a video of a three-toed sloth on the screen in front of the class. The furry creature was swimming. As the rest of the class watched it paddle through the water, Nancy leaned over to her friends.

"Tomorrow is going to be a perfect day," she said. "There's supposed to be this cool courtyard at the wildlife center with a crazy playground and a hedge maze. And there's a gift shop where you can buy stuffed animals or these pens with floating parrots in them."

"Someone said they actually put the python around your neck," George whispered. "You can hold them!"

"George!" Nancy and Bess practically screamed. Then they broke into laughter, thinking of George with a giant snake hanging over her shoulders. Sometimes the things that totally creeped them out were the same things George loved.

"I don't think we've been somewhere this fun since . . . ," Bess trailed off, her eyes wide.

"Maybe ever," George added.

Nancy smiled, knowing it was true. The River Heights Wildlife Center was going to be their biggest adventure yet.

# Chapter

2

## THE GREAT ESCAPE

"You must be Mrs. Pak, and I'm guessing these are your exceptional science students!" A woman with curly black hair bounded down the front steps of the wildlife center. She was wearing khaki from head to toe—khaki shorts, a khaki shirt, and even khaki-colored socks. Her name tag read BELINDA.

"They are," Mrs. Pak said cheerfully. "We've been so excited to visit."

"Well, come on in." The woman waved each of

them inside one by one. "I'm Belinda, and I'm the founder of the River Heights Wildlife Center. I'll be taking care of you today. Before we get started, I wanted to tell you a little bit about the place, and you can meet the wonderful staff that makes magic happen around here."

Nancy followed Bess and George inside the center, which was a single-story building with a beautiful courtyard garden in the middle of it. There were already two other school groups there. The huge playground was crowded with kids and a group of moms with strollers. Nancy could hear animal noises echoing down the corridor. To the side of the playground was the hedge maze that Nancy had read about online. Two men in khaki uniforms were standing by the café and picnic tables.

"Come, sit down!" Belinda said, waving for the class to find spots at the picnic tables. "I want to tell you a little bit about what brought me here to the River Heights Wildlife Center."

Nancy and her friends sat on the bench closest

to Belinda. She seemed like she was much younger than Nancy's parents. She had funny pins all over the front of her shirt. One said TOUCAN PLAY THAT GAME and had a cartoon drawing of a toucan. Another said TOADALLY and had an annoyed-looking toad on it.

"I'm so happy you all could come visit today, because helping animals has become my life's passion," Belinda said. "I started rescuing abandoned and injured animals when I was just a teenager. I worked in a bird sanctuary after college, and then

I came here to create the River Heights Wildlife Center."

"Are all of your animals injured?" Lily Almond, a girl with long black pigtails, asked. She was the biggest animal lover in class. Nancy had been to her house once for a school project and met her two hamsters, one bunny, three dogs, and her twenty-pound cat, Otis.

"Most of them were when they came in here," Belinda answered. "All of them needed our help. Sometimes people buy animals and they don't know what to do with them. Like our flying squirrel, Bean. Someone bought him online and didn't like how much time and effort it took to take care of him. Or our wolf, Moonrise. People actually thought he was a dog, so they brought him home, and he was trouble . . . big trouble. He tore apart two couches and ate a hole in their door."

"We learned a lot about wolves," Jamal said excitedly.

"Yes, Mrs. Pak told me all about the lessons

you've been doing lately." Belinda looked genuinely interested. "Do you know the difference between a wolf and a dog?"

"Wolves have fur on their bellies, and amber-colored eyes," Jamal said.

"And their ears stick straight up!" Lily chimed in.

"That's right," Belinda said. "We'll talk more above wolves and snakes and birds, but first I want to introduce you all to the wonderful staff here. Because we use so much of our donations to rescue and take care of our wildlife, many people who work here are volunteers. Bob has been volunteering the longest, for five years now."

A man with frizzy white hair stepped forward. He looked like he could have been someone's grandpa. "After I retired I thought it might be a fun thing to do. And I was right! I work with all the wildlife here, but I really love the capuchin monkeys. The kinkajou, too."

"The kinkajou . . . ?" Bess whispered to Nancy. Her brows furrowed.

Nancy remembered them from one of their textbooks, even though they didn't spend a lot of time talking about them. "It's like a tiny raccoon, but it's honey-colored instead of gray. And it lives in trees."

The other man stepped forward after Belinda was done talking about Bob. He had long blond hair that came down to his shoulders. He wore rings on three of his fingers, and had a goatee.

"And this is Ocean," Belinda said, introducing him. "And yes—before you ask, that is his real name."

"She tells the truth!" Ocean laughed. "My parents were hippies. I grew up on a farm in California and I've always loved wildlife, especially reptiles. I have a California king snake named Steven and a tortoise named Bette. They're two of my best friends."

"A California king," George said to no one in particular. "Very cool."

"You'll meet Lisa in the gift shop, and Miles

is coming in later," Belinda said. "Now let's start our tour, shall we? There are so many wonderful creatures here and so little time."

"Do you have pets?" Bess asked Belinda.

"I have two chinchillas at home," Belinda

said as she led the group back into the building. "I'd love to have more pets, but I take care of so many animals here, it feels like I already do. Now, where should we start . . . ?" She looked down the right hallway, then down the left. "Are you ready to meet Rainbow?"

The class cheered in response. Belinda led them to a huge enclosure with sand and shrubs in it, and fresh produce scattered everywhere. A short wood fence surrounded the perimeter.

"It looks like a cabbage exploded," Nancy whispered to Bess. "What's in there?"

"Okay everybody, find a space along the outside of the fence to look for Rainbow. She might be hard to spot at first, but look closely," Belinda directed. She waited, watching the class's faces.

Everyone lined up along the fence and peered into the enclosure.

"I see her," Lily said. Then a few more kids agreed.

Nancy narrowed her eyes and finally saw a large tortoise behind a shrub. She was all the way in the back of the habitat. Her shell was brown and dark green, so she blended in with the sand and leaves around her.

"Rainbow will always have a very special place in my heart," Belinda said, staring at the tortoise. "She was my very first rescue here at the wildlife center. An older woman had her as a pet, but when she moved she just left Rainbow in her yard with a rotting pile of vegetables. The new owners found her and, well, they called me."

Nancy stared down at the tortoise. She felt

really sad for the animal. She had to admit, it was awful that someone had just left Rainbow there all alone. What would have happened if no one found her?

"On the day I went and got her," Belinda went on, "there was the most spectacular rainbow in the sky."

"And that's how she got her name," Mrs. Pak said. She smiled, even though that part was a little obvious. It was clear Mrs. Pak loved each one of Belinda's stories.

"Desert tortoises can be between a half pound and eleven pounds, and our Rainbow is right smack in the middle," Belinda said. "She weighs just six pounds. But what she lacks in size she makes up for in personality!"

Belinda talked about how the tortoise was the longest-living animal in the world. Desert tortoises could live between fifty and eighty years, but other species could live up to one hundred and fifty years. There was even one tortoise who'd lived to two hundred and fifty years old. His name was Adwaita and he spent most of his life in a zoo in India.

Then Belinda described the tortoise shell and how it is really two connected parts. Everyone in Nancy's class loved that, because then they got to tell her everything they'd learned about tortoises over the past few weeks. Lily and Bess were shouting out answers to different questions. Bess told the whole class how desert tortoises regulate their body temperature by staying in burrows and under rocks when it's really hot outside.

"What do you think we'll see next?" George whispered, when they finally left Rainbow's enclosure and turned the corner down the great hall. Another school group was in the theater watching a short film about servals, and Nancy could tell Bess was a little jealous.

"I heard they have an alligator here," George told them.

"No way . . ." Bess suddenly looked a little scared.

The next habitat they went to wasn't open like Rainbow's. Instead, it was an enclosure with wire mesh covering all sides. It had sand and some big rocks in the back. In the corner there was a small cave that looked like it was made out of plastic.

"This is where Mo lives," Belinda said. "Mo . . . where are you? Come out, come out!" She pulled a treat from her pocket and stepped inside, closing the gate behind her. Within a few seconds a tiny red fox came out from the rocks and snatched the treat from her hand. Then it ran away.

"Did you see him? He was adorable!" Mrs. Pak laughed. Nancy had noticed how much of an animal lover Mrs. Pak was. She was always in such a good mood when she was teaching them their wildlife unit. She seemed to especially love monkeys and sloths.

Belinda told them all about the tiny kit fox and how it lived in the desert. It hid from its predators in bushes and shrubs, and ate rodents for food. When they were done, they went to the next habitat and saw two ferrets. Nancy thought they looked a little like rats, but George seemed to really like them.

"They're kind of funny," George whispered.

"Now I have a special surprise for you," Belinda said, turning a corner to another habitat. It was open and had a giant tree in the middle, with branches that touched the ceiling. She disappeared into a back room and came out with a furry baby clinging to her arm. "I want you to meet Peanut!"

"Is that a sloth?" Bess asked. "A baby sloth?"

Nancy hadn't seen Mrs. Pak so happy since their class had won first place in the River Heights Science Olympics. Both her hands were covering her mouth.

"Come on in," Belinda said, waving the class inside. "This is one of our interactive habitats. Who would like to hold Peanut first? Just be very gentle with her, she scares easily."

Jamal's hand shot into the air. Belinda laid the tiny sloth down across his chest, and he held on to Peanut with both hands.

Nancy and her friends crowded around the furry sloth. Its eyes were half closed, like it might fall asleep at any moment. It had a long snout, and each of its paws had three long claws on them.

"Peanut was born here in our wildlife center," Belinda said. "Her mom, Luna, came in when she was just about to give birth. We like to think of her as the baby of our quirky family, because we have so few of those around here. Most of our animals are much older."

"Doesn't algae grow on sloth's fur?" Jamal

asked, remembering the fact from one of Mrs. Pak's lessons. He never took his eyes off the tiny creature in his arms.

"It does! What a great bit of knowledge," Belinda said. "Most sloths are from Costa Rica, and algae can grow on their fur because of the humidity there They hang upside down in trees, and because of that green algae, they look more like a bundle of leaves than an animal. It's the perfect camouflage."

Nancy turned around to say something to Bess, and that's when she noticed the other wildlife volunteer standing in the hall. It was Bob, the older man with white hair. He looked like he was trying to get Belinda's attention, but now she was moving the sloth into Lily's arms. She started talking to Lily about how sloths were great swimmers.

After a few minutes, Belinda finally noticed him and handed Peanut to Mrs. Pak. "Would you mind watching the little guys while I'm gone?"

Mrs. Pak laughed. "Mind? I'd be delighted!" She took Peanut into her arms.

Belinda walked outside the habitat to meet Bob, and the two of them walked down the hall. Nancy stepped away from the group but she still couldn't hear what they were saying.

"He looks really worried," Bess whispered. "What do you think it's about?"

Nancy watched them from the edge of the sloth habitat. Bob kept wringing his hands together. The rest of the class was chatting about sloths and Costa Rica, but after a few minutes they seemed to realize something was wrong too. A few of the kids stepped out of the habitat to see where Belinda went.

"What's wrong?" Mrs. Pak asked, when Belinda finally came back. Belinda was rubbing her forehead with her fingers, like she had a bad headache. Peanut, the baby sloth, was still curled around Mrs. Pak's hand.

"It's Rainbow," Belinda said, her voice uneven. "She's missing!"

# Chapter

## AN UNLIKELY SUSPECT

Belinda put Peanut back and ushered the class out of the sloth exhibit.

"Okay, guys, quick detour," she said. "We're going back to Rainbow's enclosure to see if we can find where's she hiding." Belinda smiled and put them all at ease. Rainbow wasn't lost, they just had to find her!

Everyone lined up single file and followed Belinda and Bob back to the tortoise exhibit in the Reptile Hall. *Tortoises are so slow*, Nancy thought, *so there's no way Rainbow could have escaped.*

"Okay, guys. Everyone line up around the enclosure just like last time," Belinda told them. "Look around and see if you can find her again!"

"She was right there!" Bob said, once they had all found a place around the fence. He pointed to a spot on the ground. "She was eating a carrot when I last saw her. That couldn't have been more than twenty or thirty minutes ago." Bob was a lot less calm than Belinda.

"She must be around here somewhere," Belinda said. "I'll go into the enclosure to look behind some of the rocks and things. After all, she couldn't have gotten far. . . ."

"Maybe she escaped." Mark, one of Nancy's classmates, smirked. He seemed to like the idea of an escape artist turtle.

"Could she have climbed over the fence though?" Mrs. Pak was studying the two-foot-high wooden beams that surrounded the habitat. "It seems unlikely."

"No, I don't think she would." Belinda walked

into the habitat and checked under a short shrub in the front corner. "This was one of her favorite hiding spots."

"I'm so sorry, Belinda. . . ." Bob shook his head. "I really am. I was in charge of the Reptile Hall today, and I can't believe this happened on my watch."

"It's okay, Bob. She could still be in here somewhere," Bess assured him. "We just have to keep looking."

Nancy could tell he was taking this pretty personally. His eyes looked watery, like he was fighting back tears.

Then Nancy heard the sounds of sneakers squeaking on tiles coming from down the hallway and looked up to see a woman running toward them.

The woman had a baby strapped to her chest and she kept stopping to look under benches and in different enclosures. "Abby! Abby, where are you? This isn't funny anymore," she called out. "If you come out I'll give you a candy bar!"

She stopped outside of Rainbow's enclosure.
"I've been looking all over for you," she said.
She was waving to a little girl who was coming

out from behind a huge rock in the back corner. "You're not supposed to be wandering around by yourself! And what are you doing in there, of all places?"

The young mother stomped into the habitat and grabbed Abby by the hand. She didn't seem to notice Belinda until she was on her way out. "I'm so sorry," the mom said. "She has a habit of getting into trouble."

"I just wanted to see the turtle!" Abby whined.

Nancy glanced sideways at Bess and George. She just wanted to see the turtle? Abby was talking about Rainbow. She had run away from her mother right around the time the tortoise went missing. Was this little girl their first real suspect?

"Did you end up seeing the turtle?" Nancy asked. "The one that was right here, where you were hiding?"

Abby suddenly seemed nervous. She grabbed her mother's hand and slipped behind her legs.

"We're only asking because our tortoise,

Rainbow, just went missing," Belinda explained to the young mother. The woman was tall with dark bangs that kept falling in her eyes. "If your daughter saw anything . . . or maybe she let her out of the enclosure or hid her somewhere—"

"Are you saying that my daughter, my Abby, stole your turtle?" The woman looked at Mrs. Pak's class like she wanted them to take her side. "You have got to be kidding me! She's six years old!"

"But she was here when Rainbow disappeared, wasn't she? Rainbow's not very big. Anyone could pick her up," Bob chimed in. He narrowed his eyes at the little girl. "If you took the tortoise, you have to tell us right now. This is very serious. We'll have to call security."

The little girl stared up at them, her brown eyes wide. Then her chin started to tremble. She let out the loudest, most sorrowful cry, and buried her sobbing face in her mother's side.

# Chapter

## DOUBLE TAKES

Belinda tried to comfort the crying child, but it wasn't much use. Her sobs echoed through the corridor. Nancy and her friends made their way to Mrs. Pak, who was standing awkwardly with the rest of the class, unsure what to do.

"Mrs. Pak . . . I know we could help if they let us," Nancy said as she stepped aside with her teacher. "Abby's just scared because of the way Bob spoke to her. But she was there at the same time Rainbow went missing. She could've seen something."

Mrs. Pak seemed to like the idea. "You three are pretty great at solving mysteries. I still can't believe you found my missing ruby ring in September. That was incredible."

Nancy just shrugged, like it was no big deal. The ring had fallen into the heating grate underneath Mrs. Pak's desk. They investigated the possibility someone had taken it, but it wasn't long before they realized that wasn't the case.

"Excuse me, Belinda . . . ," Mrs. Pak said, taking Nancy, Bess, and George to the front of the group. "I want you to meet Nancy Drew, Bess Marvin, and George Fayne. These three girls have solved half the mysteries in River Heights. They've got quite a talent for it."

Abby stopped crying when Nancy and her friends came over. She seemed just as interested in what Mrs. Pak was saying as Belinda was. Belinda furrowed her brows, a little confused.

"I know we're young, but we've got a lot of experience with this kind of thing. Stolen purses, unexplained pranks, missing dogs—you name it," Nancy jumped in. She was used to people underestimating them at first, but she never let that stop her.

"Well . . . ," Belinda tilted her head to the side, considering it. "If you think—"

"But they're just kids!" Bob said. "No offense girls, but this is really serious. Rainbow could be in real danger."

"We know," George said. Nancy could tell she was annoyed. "We'd love to talk to Abby and her mom for a minute, just to see if they noticed anything strange."

"It's worth a shot," Belinda shrugged. "Why don't you do a little investigating while I finish the tour with your class. If you find out anything, I promise you can come back to River Heights Wildlife Center anytime you like, and I'll show you anything you might have missed. And even if you don't find out anything, the offer still stands."

"I'm going to do some of my own investigating too," Bob jumped in. He crossed his arms over his chest and frowned. Nancy had changed her mind about him. He didn't look like someone's grandpa—he looked like someone's mean grandpa.

Belinda glanced at her watch. "You can have until the end of the day, and then I think I need to call the police and report her stolen. I hope you can find our girl," she said. "And for the rest of Mrs. Pak's class—let's head back toward the sloth exhibit."

Belinda gave Nancy a half smile on her way out, and Mrs. Pak mouthed the words "good luck!" Soon Nancy and the Clue Crew were standing alone with Abby and her mom.

"I'm Nancy," Nancy said, sticking out her hand. "And this is Bess and George."

"I'm Candace," Abby's mom said. She seemed to calm down now that Abby had stopped crying. "Do you mind if we sit down at one of those picnic tables in the courtyard? I can only do this for so long. . . ."

She pointed to the baby who was strapped to her chest. The baby had somehow slept through the entire scene, a big cotton hat covering its eyes.

"No problem," Nancy said, leading them outside to a table far away from the rest of the class. As soon as they sat down, another woman with a stroller came over.

"Candace—what's going on? What happened?" the woman asked. Her long blond hair was tied up in a bun, and she kept looking from Nancy to Candace, then from Candace to Nancy.

"Oh, come sit down Beth, please. These girls just want to ask Abby some questions about a turtle that went missing . . . long story." Candace kept shaking her head as Beth sat down beside her.

"Did you see the tortoise when you were wandering around looking at animals?" Nancy asked, looking at Abby. The girl just shook her head. "Are you sure?"

"This is a little ridiculous," Candace snapped. "Abby didn't have anything to do with this. She may wander off sometimes, but she doesn't steal things!"

Candace's friend Beth nodded in agreement. "Or animals," she added.

"I didn't see the turtle!" Abby finally said, but her cheeks were pink. Nancy could tell she was hiding something . . . but what? She thought it would be better now that Bob wasn't there to scare her, but Abby still seemed nervous.

"We just had to ask to be sure," Bess chimed in.

"What's that in your pocket?" George said, pointing to a weird outline on the front of Abby's shorts. Nancy had noticed it, but she hadn't thought to ask.

Abby's chin started to tremble again. "What is it?" Candace asked, reaching for it, and pulled it out. It took Nancy a moment to realize it was a piece of chocolate wrapped in colorful paper. "Is this from the gift shop? Did you take this from the gift shop?" Candace asked.

Abby started crying all over again. She stuck her face in her mom's side. "I'm sorry, I shouldn't have, Mommy."

Candace sighed. "So she took a candy from

the gift shop. We'll give it back. Now, does that clear things up?" She was looking at Nancy, George, and Bess like this was all somehow their fault. "I just don't get why you're talking to us when that weird boy was walking around alone. He was definitely up to something—why don't you go find him?"

Nancy glanced sideways at her friends. A boy? What boy?

"Oh, I saw that kid too," Beth added. "He passed our group at least two times. He was just walking around by himself. Kind of suspicious. Had on a striped shirt."

"Wait . . ." Candace shook her head. "I thought he was wearing a white T-shirt, or maybe it was gray. Didn't he have on white high-top sneakers?"

"You're talking about the kid, he had a button nose and freckles?" Beth asked.

"Yeah, that's him," Candace agreed. "He was definitely wearing a white T-shirt. He had big blue eyes."

"Yes. Big blue eyes . . . and a striped shirt."

Beth shot her friend a look as if to say *you've got this all wrong.*

Nancy pulled her clue book from her knapsack and started writing down everything the women had said. It wasn't unusual for witnesses to disagree on what a suspect looked like. She wrote that the boy had blue eyes and a button nose. "Freckles," she added, remembering what else they'd agreed on.

"What color hair did he have?" Bess asked.

"I think light," Beth said.

"Yeah, light," Candace agreed.

"Can you remember anything else about him?" George asked. "How old was he? A teenager?"

Just then the baby who was strapped to Candace's chest woke up. It squirmed a little in its carrier, then let out a loud wail.

Candace stood and started bouncing it up and down, but it just cried louder. Everyone in the courtyard turned to look.

"We have to go," she said, grabbing Abby's hand. Beth followed her out, saying something about having diapers in her car. "Good luck!" she called over her shoulder, then they were gone.

Nancy and her friends took off across the courtyard and found a quiet bench where they could talk. "They're definitely describing the same boy," Nancy said, looking at her notes in the clue book. "I wish we could've found out a bit more, though. I mean . . . a boy could be five or fifteen to them. And they couldn't even agree on what he was wearing. I must've seen half a dozen boys wearing stripes today, and even more wearing white T-shirts."

"Is it possible he changed clothes at some point?" Bess asked.

"If he's the one who took Rainbow, it's possible," George said.

Nancy sighed, feeling more stumped than she

had in a while. She could definitely see a teenage boy wanting a tortoise as a pet. But even when descriptions of suspects were different, they usually weren't this different. Something strange was going on. . . .

"If he did change his clothes to hide his identity," she finally said, "we're dealing with one of our sneakiest suspects yet."

# Chapter

## ONE LAST LOOK

"Over here!" Bess called out. "Look at this." She was leaning over a footprint in the sand. From what Nancy could tell, it seemed like it was from a sneaker.

They'd returned to Rainbow's habitat to see if they'd missed any clues when they were first there. Nancy had looked under every shrub and branch but hadn't found a thing.

"It's a print . . . and it's not ours," Bess said. "And it's not Belinda's or Bob's, either. Did you

notice? They both wear boots. With thick soles so they can walk right through mud and sand and twigs."

"And Abby and her mom were only on that side," George added, pointing to the other end of the enclosure. Candace had only taken a few steps in the sand. "It isn't theirs, either."

"So why would a person wearing sneakers be in here, if the workers all wear boots?" Nancy asked, though she knew the answer. Whoever came in may have been the one to steal Rainbow.

George came up behind them and stared at the footprint too. One of the other school groups walked past, and Nancy couldn't help but scan the group, looking for boys in striped shirts. "It's definitely an adult's footprint though. So what about the kid Candace and Beth described?"

"There might be a connection between them," Bess tried. "Or maybe the kid is the real witness, the way we thought Abby might be."

Nancy took another lap around the habitat, checking the perimeter. Belinda was right, there weren't any holes in it. It would've been almost impossible for Rainbow to have gotten out on her own.

Nancy wandered into the back room, where Belinda stored a lot of the supplies for the different animals. There was a small fridge and some cabinets and food bins. Inside the fridge was a basket of strawberries, a few heads of lettuce, and two small bottles with Rainbow's name on them. Nancy picked up the bottles and studied them.

"All of her food is still here, and so is Rainbow's medicine," she said, reading the label on one of the bottles. "It says she needs to take it twice a day. But whoever has her didn't bring it with them."

"That rules out a lot of people who work here," Bess said. "They would've known she needed the medicine, and they would've thought to take it with them."

Nancy flipped the clue book back open. "Why

would someone want Rainbow?" She wrote "POSSIBLE MOTIVES," and underlined it.

"To keep her as a pet," Bess said. "Or worst case . . . to sell her."

Nancy wrote both down. The thought of someone selling Rainbow made her really sad. Belinda loved Rainbow so much. She would be devastated if someone sold her off to anyone with the money to buy her.

"Hey . . . where'd George go?" Bess asked, looking around. Nancy tucked away the clue book.

They finally spotted George on the other side of the Reptile Hall. They went over to her, but she hardly seemed to notice them. She was staring at the chameleon exhibit. Behind the glass were two chameleons sitting by some leaves. They walked onto a branch and they both turned a light shade of brown.

"Chameleons?" Nancy asked. "Why are you looking at these guys?"

Nancy thought chameleons had cute faces,

but she didn't see how they had anything to do with the mystery they were trying to solve.

"They look exactly the same . . . like twins." George turned to them, her brown eyes bright. "I got it! I know the boy Candace was talking about!"

# Chapter

## A MAZE OF CLUES

"It's Harry and Liam!" George said. "Don't you see? Who else would look exactly the same, but be wearing different clothes?"

Nancy flipped through the clue book and nodded. "Twins . . . you're right. They both have blue eyes, freckles, and button noses. Light hair, too!"

"And doesn't Liam have white high-top sneakers?" Bess added.

"I think so . . . ," Nancy said. "We should go find them. I bet the class is still in the courtyard!"

The girls ran down the corridor and turned in to the courtyard garden. About half the class was still sitting at the picnic tables with Mrs. Pak, eating their bag lunches. Mrs. Pak looked excited to see them.

"Did you find anything?" she asked.

"Kind of . . . Do you know where Harry and Liam are?" Bess replied. "We need to talk to them."

"I think they're playing tag over there," Lily pointed to the playground by the hedge maze, then took another bite of her sandwich. There was a sign by the slide that said ENCHANTED PLAYGROUND in giant letters. The whole place was designed to look like it was inside an overgrown garden. Huge plastic tulips and roses towered over the swings.

Nancy and her friends thanked them and took off toward the playground. The twins were on the monkey bars. They both swung across, rung by rung, until Nancy called out to them. "Liam, Harry—can we talk to you?"

Harry jumped off the monkey bars and Liam followed, landing in the gravel below. Harry was in a green-and-white striped shirt and Liam was wearing a white T-shirt and white high-top sneakers. They both seemed a little shocked to see Nancy, Bess, and George.

"Hey, guys!" Bess waved as the girls got closer. "We just have a couple of questions to ask you." But they hadn't taken more than a few steps when Harry and Liam sprinted away. They turned into the hedge maze, disappearing inside.

"Well, that's suspicious," Bess said.

"They're up to something!" George said, chasing after them.

Nancy and Bess followed, but ran into a fork in the path.

"Which way did they go?" Bess asked.

"No idea," Nancy admitted. "Let's split up. Then one of us is sure to find them."

Bess gave Nancy a determined nod and rushed off to the left. Nancy headed for the right fork.

Nancy went deeper into the maze, where the

tall green bushes were on all sides of her so she couldn't see anything beyond them. Nancy turned right, then right again, then left, but everything looked the same. She was totally lost!

Luckily, she could rely on her other senses. And soon enough she could hear laughter in the distance. Could it be the twins? Did Bess find George?

"Bess!! George??" Nancy called out. Somewhere in the distance she thought she heard George say something, but she couldn't figure out what. She was too far away.

Nancy kept running through the maze, until eventually she hit a dead end. Just when she thought she'd never find her way out, she saw a flash of green and white sprint by her. She ran after the twins, winding through the hedge until she finally cornered them in another one of the maze's dead ends. Harry looked around, realizing they were completely trapped.

"It was all his idea!" he said, pointing at his brother. "I didn't even want to do it!"

Within seconds, George and Bess appeared behind Nancy. They must've heard Harry yelling and found her.

"I knew it," George said, still trying to catch her breath. "Now just tell us where Rainbow is and everything will be okay. Belinda just wants her back."

Liam's scrunched his nose. "Rainbow?" he asked. "You mean the turtle?"

"The tortoise," Bess corrected him. "We want her back. Now."

Harry started laughing. "We didn't steal her! We thought you found the mealworms."

Once Harry started laughing he couldn't stop. He was doubled over, and that made Liam start laughing too. It took them a while before they could even speak. "We just . . . ," Liam tried to say. "We were going to play this really big prank. We got some mealworms from the hedgehog enclosure and we put them in a few of the girls' backpacks."

"I wanted to see the look on Lily's face when she pulled out a handful of bugs!" Harry laughed.

"That's not funny," George said. "It's just gross. Are you trying to impress Antonio again? He's been doing stuff like that for years. That's definitely not going to impress him."

Harry and Liam didn't seem to like that. They suddenly looked much more serious than before. "But they're mealworms. . . ." Liam trailed off. "They're little and weird. It is funny."

Nancy didn't care about the mealworms in her bag, or Liam and Harry's silly prank. But she did care about when they'd been playing it.

"When exactly were you wandering around the wildlife center looking for mealworms? You must've snuck away from the group. But when?" Nancy asked.

Liam shrugged. "I don't know. Pretty much right after we saw the fox."

"We came back when Belinda brought that baby sloth out," Harry added. "That was super cool. Everyone was oohing and ahhhing over all the animals. No one seemed to notice we were gone."

Nancy raised her eyebrows at her friends. Candace and Beth had been right, the twins were wandering around the wildlife center at the same exact time Rainbow went missing. Of course they thought they'd had something to do with it.

But Nancy knew better. They weren't suspects. . . . Harry and Liam were witnesses.

# Chapter

# A MYSTERIOUS NOTE

Nancy and her friends followed Harry and Liam through the hedge maze. The boys had already gone through it twice before, so they were a little better at figuring out where the exits were. It wasn't long before they all made their way back to the playground.

"Just think," Bess said. "Did you see anything odd when you were walking around the center? Does anything stand out to you?"

Harry scratched his head. "I don't think so. . . ."

"Yeah." Liam shrugged. "I don't know."

"It might be the smallest detail," George added.

"Oh, there was this guy with a duffel bag," Harry finally said. He sat down on the bottom of the slide, ignoring the toddler at the top waiting for her turn. "Do you remember, Liam?"

"I don't think I saw him." Liam shook his head.

Nancy pulled out the clue book to write down everything Harry said.

"I only noticed him because he was going out this side door, like, not the normal exit," Harry continued. "And I remember the bag because it seemed like it was moving. I couldn't really say anything because we were trying to sneak back to the group."

"A moving bag?" Bess smiled. "That does sound suspicious."

Nancy couldn't help but smile too. This felt like the best lead they'd had so far. It was very possible Rainbow was in that bag, and the guy

Harry was describing was their prime suspect.

"Tell us everything you can remember," Nancy said.

"I didn't see his face, and I don't really remember what he was wearing," Harry went on. "His back was facing me. But that bag was definitely moving!"

"What did the bag look like?" Bess asked. "Do you remember what color it was?"

"Oh! It had that on it!" Harry pointed somewhere behind them. They turned and saw the logo for the River Heights Wildlife Center right above the back exit. It had a picture of a sloth with a circle around it, then the words RIVER HEIGHTS WILDLIFE CENTER around the outside of the circle.

"The logo for the center?" George asked.

"Yeah, it was a green bag and it had that sign on it," Harry said. "That's all I really remember."

"Thanks for your help, Harry," Nancy said. "And before the end of the day, you two should really fish those mealworms out of our bags, or I'm going to have to tell Mrs. Pak who was responsible for that."

Liam crossed his arms over his chest, like he was not pleased. Nancy couldn't really worry about him, or Harry, because they had to find the guy with the duffel bag. And she had a pretty good idea where they should start looking. . . .

The gift shop was packed with souvenirs. There was a whole wall of stuffed animals. A row of koala bears hung from a fake tree branch and stuffed wolves were lurking around the small store. Bess picked up a snow globe that had an artic fox inside. She swirled it around to kick up the white flakes.

"There it is," George said, pointing to a spinning rack in the corner of the store.

Forest-green duffel bags hung off it. They all had the same River Heights Wildlife Center logo.

"Do you think he'd buy the duffel bag from the store, just to use it to carry Rainbow out?" Nancy asked. It didn't quite add up to her, but it was a possibility.

"Maybe he bought it earlier," Bess said. "Maybe weeks before."

Nancy picked up one of the bags and brought it to the register. A woman with a long brown braid was working. Her name tag said LISA. "Hi, Lisa," Nancy said. "We're helping Belinda out today and trying to find Rainbow, the missing tortoise."

"Oh! Bob was just in here telling me all about it." Lisa's green eyes went wide. "He's really upset."

"I know," Nancy went on. "That's why we were wondering if you could help us. Do you have a record of all the times the store sold this duffel bag in the last month? We think whoever took Rainbow might've used this to carry her out."

"That's terrible," Lisa said. "But I'm afraid

we don't keep records like that. Not for a whole month. I can tell you no one bought that bag today, because I've been working since nine o'clock, when the center opened."

"Dead end," Bess whispered. She leaned on the counter, her chin in her hands.

"I wish I could help more," Lisa said. "I don't remember selling that bag to anyone recently. They're not really flying off the shelves, but we do give them to all the volunteers when they start."

"Does that mean you're the one who stole Rainbow?" George joked.

"Don't look at me!" Lisa laughed, holding both her hands up in the air. "I was here all morning. You can check the store security camera. And I don't think Bob has it in him either. Ocean has his own tortoise at home, so he's out too. I really don't think this was an inside job."

Nancy nodded at the phrase "inside job." She'd heard it before to describe when someone working at a place committed a crime. It seemed like a very adult thing to say.

"Do you have a list of volunteers we could look at?" Nancy asked. "Maybe we could rule some people out. . . ."

Lisa leaned under the counter and pulled out a clipboard with some papers on it. She flipped through them and showed Nancy the last page. There were about thirty volunteers who came to the center throughout each month. It would be impossible to investigate each one by four o'clock.

As Nancy and Bess read through the list of

names, someone ran into the store behind them. Nancy turned to see Bob holding a crumpled piece of paper. Belinda was trailing behind him, a worried look on her face.

"You're not going to believe what I found!" he said, waving the paper in the air. "It's a ransom note!"

# Chapter

8

## THE SMALLEST DETAILS

He put it on the counter, smoothing down the edges. Belinda, Lisa, Nancy, and her friends all circled around it, trying to get a better look. As soon as Nancy read it, she realized Bob was exaggerating. It wasn't a ransom note because it didn't demand any money or anything in exchange for the tortoise. But it was a note from whoever took Rainbow, which made Nancy think they were on the right track.

"'Do not worry about Rainbow,'" Bess read.

"'She will have a good life and I'll take good care of her.'"

Belinda flipped the note over, making sure it didn't say anything else. "That's it?" she said, annoyed. "That's supposed to make me feel better? Who is this person?"

Nancy read the note over again, looking for clues. "Well, whoever wrote this obviously cares a lot about her," she said. That means it wasn't a stranger, or someone who didn't understand animals. She was starting to think maybe it was someone from the volunteer list.

"They also care a lot about what people here think," Bess added. "They wouldn't have sent you all a note if they weren't worried that you were worried. A stranger would've just run away and never thought about it again."

"And it's one person," George added, pointing to the wording. "It's not two people, or a group working together. They said, 'I'll take good care of her.'"

"Does that handwriting seem familiar to

you?" Nancy asked Bob and Belinda.

Belinda just shrugged. "Maybe, but I don't know. . . . But it does kind of look familiar."

Nancy thought about Rainbow's habitat. The fridge in the back had all her food and her medicine. She smiled, an idea forming. . . .

"Okay, so if the person who took her cares a lot about her," Nancy said, "they're not going to leave her medicine behind. We need to go quick—they might be there already!"

"Wait! Where are you going?" Bob called out as the girls ran out of the store. He seemed worried that they were going to solve the mystery before he did. "Go where quick?"

Nancy turned and waved to Belinda as they left. "We're close! Don't worry, I have a good feeling about this!"

# Chapter

## WAIT AND SEE

Nancy, Bess, and George raced through the wild-life center, toward Rainbow's habitat. As they turned the corner, Nancy was half expecting to see someone emerging from the enclosure, but it was still empty. She went right to the back room, circling the small refrigerator, but no one was there.

Nancy opened the refrigerator. "The medicine is still here." Everything was exactly as they'd left it. Even the basket of strawberries hadn't been touched. "If it is who I think it is, they'll be here any moment."

"You have a strong feeling about someone?" Bess asked. "Me too."

"I wonder if we're right," George said.

"We should hide. Do a real stakeout," Nancy said. She loved having stakeouts with Bess and George. It was when you waited for a suspect to return to the scene of a crime, or a particular place. Nancy was sure that whoever came back for Rainbow's medicine would be the same person who took her.

Nancy glanced around the room, searching for somewhere to hide. There were mostly storage bins and cabinets for supplies. Nancy opened the biggest cabinet and found bins of gravel and fake branches that were used in the different reptile exhibits. She crouched down on the bottom shelf, leaving one door open a crack so she could still peer out. Bess ducked behind a giant bin of carrot tops and George hid behind the door, so that when it opened she'd be completely hidden.

George switched off the lights so it was harder to
see them.

They stayed perfectly still. They waited . . . and
waited some more. Nancy was bent over and her
back started hurting. She didn't know how much
longer she could stay squished into the bottom of
the cabinet.

She was starting to rethink her hiding spot when the door opened, lighting up the room. A tall figure in a baseball cap and sunglasses tiptoed to the refrigerator and opened it, their face glowing in the light. They were wearing a baggy sweatshirt over their clothes to disguise their identity. They reached down and grabbed the bottle of medicine from the top shelf and tucked it in their pocket. Then they turned to leave.

George sprang out from behind the door and switched on the light. Bess rose up from her spot behind the storage bin and Nancy opened the cabinet, stepping into the room.

"Stop right there!" Nancy said in her scariest you-better-listen-to-me voice. "We know you have Rainbow!"

# Clue Crew—and
# YOU!

Join Nancy, Bess, and George in solving this mystery. Or turn the page to find out whodunit!

1. Nancy, Bess, and George ruled out Abby and the twins. We know the suspect cares about animals and the people who work at the Wildlife Center. Who else could have taken Rainbow? List your suspects on a piece of paper.

2. The Clue Crew interviewed a lot of people on this case. They talked to Abby's mom, the twins, and Lisa. Who else could they have interviewed? Write down your thoughts on a piece of paper.

3. Nancy, Bess, and George studied Rainbow's enclosure for clues, and they found a footprint that could lead them to the tortoise taker. They also noticed the medicine hadn't been taken. What else do you think they could have looked for? Make a list of your ideas on a piece of paper.

# Chapter

10

## BESTIE FOR BETTE

Ocean froze with the bottle of medicine in his hand. After he realized he was caught, he pulled off his baseball cap and sunglasses and put them in the front pocket of his hoodie.

Nancy stared down at his sneakers. He didn't wear boots like Belinda or Bob, but an old pair of tennis shoes. Nancy glanced sideways at her friends, seeing if they had noticed too. Bess's eyes were wide. Ocean's shoes were the type of sneakers that had made the footprint in Rainbow's habitat. It all lined up.

"I can explain, I swear," Ocean said, his cheeks bright pink.

"You should, then," George replied. "Everyone was so worried about Rainbow. Belinda thought she'd never see her again."

Ocean put his face in his hands. He took a few deep breaths, as if he was trying to calm himself down. If Nancy hadn't known how much confusion and panic he'd caused, she would've felt more sorry for him.

"I'm not a bad guy, really," Ocean tried. He sat down on the floor, leaning his back against the wall. "I've been volunteering at the wildlife center for three months now. And just two weeks after I started there was that huge rainstorm. Remember the one that knocked down the tree on Main Street?"

Nancy nodded. It had been a big story in River Heights. There was thunder and lighting and rain that came at you sideways. Their neighbor's car had to get fixed after a giant branch fell on it.

"What does a rainstorm have to do with Rainbow?" Nancy asked.

"Well, that night of the rainstorm, the wildlife center got a leak in the roof, right above Rainbow's habitat," Ocean continued. "There was this huge gross puddle right in the middle of her home, and they needed to fix the roof and clean everything up. So Rainbow had nowhere to go. We were going to keep her in the back room, but we knew she'd be miserable there. She's used to crawling around and having free reign over the place."

"But you have a tortoise habitat at home . . . ," Bess said, putting it together. "For your tortoise, Bette."

"Exactly!" Ocean said. He seemed to brighten up at that, as if Bess understood him completely. "So I was trying to be nice, and I said Rainbow could stay with Bette for a few days while the roof was getting fixed. And Belinda was so relieved, because she knows how great I am with Bette.

It's one of the reasons I wanted to volunteer at the center—I really love animals."

"If you love animals so much, why would take one away from her home?" George asked. She crossed her arms over her chest. Nancy could tell she was still not liking Ocean's story.

"Well, that's just it," Ocean replied, brushing his long blond hair out of his eyes. "When I took Rainbow back to my house, she loved being with Bette, and Bette loved being with her. I'd never seen either of them so happy. And I know what you're thinking: How can you tell if a tortoise is happy? Well I can. And that's when I realized— Rainbow was home. With Bette. With us."

"Did you tell Belinda about it?" Nancy asked. "She just wants Rainbow to be happy. She loves her so much, I'm sure she would understand."

"That's the thing," Ocean said, holding up a finger. "I did tell her. As soon as those three days were up, I brought Rainbow back to the center and I told Belinda everything. How Rainbow was eating more, and how she was more active, and how her and Bette liked to hang out in the same corner of the enclosure. They were so excited just to have a friend. But Belinda didn't want to hear it. She's so attached to Rainbow because Rainbow was the first animal she rescued for the center. It's part of her whole story. I knew there was no way she'd ever let her go."

"But did you ask her if Rainbow could come and live with you?" George asked.

"I did! I said, 'You know, Rainbow could always come live with Bette if she'd be happier here,'" Ocean said. "I really tried. The worst part is, Bette has been depressed ever since. It's heartbreaking to watch. She just mopes around, and now I can see how sad Rainbow is too. I didn't think I'd be hurting anyone, not really . . . and I know I didn't go about it the right way . . . but I just wanted to help. . . ."

Nancy let out a deep breath. She was starting to understand where Ocean was coming from. No matter how wrong it was to steal a tortoise from the center, he didn't think he was actually stealing Rainbow. He thought he was saving her.

"I know it's hard, but you're going to have to tell Belinda everything that happened, and why," Nancy started. "And of course, Rainbow has to come back here to live at the center. Where is she now?"

"I brought her home on my break," Ocean said. "She's with Bette. They're together."

"Well, you'll have to bring her back as soon as possible," Nancy went on. She went to the door and gave Ocean her hand, helping him to stand up. Bess and George walked out of the room, and they trailed behind them into the Reptile Hall. "Come on. If you leave now you can be back before we head home. . . ."

It took Ocean half an hour to get back to the River Heights Wildlife Center with Rainbow. He placed her gently back into her habitat and watched as she crawled toward a pile of strawberries. For a moment Nancy was worried he might cry.

Bess came down the hall with Belinda and Bob. Bob's eyebrows were knitted together, and his cheeks were bright red, like he might start yelling at any second. "Where is she?" he asked, his voice booming.

"She's here, she's okay," George said, pointing into the habitat.

"Well, I should hope she's okay!" Bob cried.

Belinda stared down at the tortoise, then leveled her eyes at Ocean. She looked so serious, it was such a change from how she'd greeted them that morning. "Please, explain this to me. I really want to understand."

"I'm so sorry Belinda . . . ," Ocean said, and this time his eyes really did fill with tears. He went through the whole story, telling her that he knew he didn't go about things the right way, but he really was just thinking of Bette and Rainbow. He also went into a long, weird tangent about animals, and how he believed they were unique souls.

"I just didn't know what to do," Ocean said. "It was like you didn't even hear what I was saying. You were never going to let Rainbow leave the center," Ocean continued.

"Of course she wasn't!" Bob snapped. "This is Rainbow's home. This is where she belongs."

Belinda tilted her head to the side, considering everything that Ocean had said. After a long while she finally spoke. "It's not an excuse, Ocean," she said. "What you did was wrong, even if your intentions were good. But you were right when you said I couldn't hear that suggestion. I love Rainbow like she's my own pet, and it's hard for me to think about her not being here every day when I walk in the door."

"I'm glad she's back," she continued. "I am. And I'll think about your suggestion. Maybe Bette can come visit Rainbow here at the center every weekend. That might work. And we could see how it goes. Maybe there are other options we can explore, keeping Bette and Rainbow's happiness in mind."

Ocean's face brightened. He smiled, relieved. "That would be great. She'd love that."

"But I'm afraid you'll have to stop volunteering at the center," Belinda went on. "You've broken my trust, and that's no small thing. We'd love to have you as a visitor whenever you like. Just say the word."

Ocean dabbed at his eyes and nodded. "I understand."

Nancy's stomach twisted in a knot. She knew it was the right decision, and it was what Belinda had to do, but it was still a little sad that Ocean wouldn't be able to come back to work. She wished none of this had happened in the first place.

"As for you girls," Belinda said, glancing at her watch, "it's almost time for you to head back to school. You should all meet me in the gift shop for a special surprise.

Belinda turned and went back down the hall, Bob following right behind her. He muttered something that sounded like "Unbelievable!" It was only then that Nancy had the courage to say what she was thinking out loud.

"If there hadn't been that leak," she said, "Bette and Rainbow wouldn't have met. None of this would have ever happened, and you would still be able to work here."

"No," Ocean said. "I wouldn't have wanted that. I'm glad they met because now they can be happy together. Even if that means Bette spends more time here than she does at home. I wouldn't trade that for anything."

Nancy, Bess, and George said their goodbyes to Ocean, though George still didn't feel that bad for him. He was responsible for his own actions, and he'd chosen to do what he did.

They walked down the long hall toward the gift shop, where Mrs. Pak was waiting with their friends.

"Nancy!" Lily called out. "Belinda is giving us all a special treat because you found Rainbow!"

Lily held up a giant lollipop with swirling greens and blues in it. It was covered in a plastic wrapper that had the River Heights Wildlife Center logo on it. Nancy glanced around, realizing all of her classmates were holding one.

"And these are for you," Belinda said, handing Nancy, Bess, and George one. "It's a small token to say thank you. But I want you to know, any time you come here you'll be given the VIP treatment. Just ask for me and I'll give you a private tour. You missed so much of today because you were solving this mystery for us. I want you to enjoy yourselves the next time you're here."

Mrs. Pak patted Nancy on the back, prouder than ever. "You did well, girls." She laughed. "Now come on, we have to get on the bus."

All of Nancy's classmates came over and

congratulated them, giving them high fives and a few cheers. Harry and Liam said they took all the mealworms out of the girls' backpacks, and told Nancy they thought what she did was "really cool." It seemed like they were starting to be more impressed with the Clue Crew than they were with Antonio Elefano.

As Nancy and her friends trailed behind the

group, they heard a familiar voice call out behind them. "Nancy! Wait one minute!"

They turned to see Bob with a huge smile on his face. He stepped toward them and gave them a tiny bow, like they were royalty. "I just wanted to say thank you," he said. "And you were right. I never should have doubted you."

"No, you shouldn't have," Nancy laughed. "And you're welcome."

Then they left for the bus, waving at him before they slipped out the door.

Test your detective skills with even more Clue Book mysteries:

# Nancy Drew Clue Book #12: Turkey Trot Plot

CAROLYN KEENE · PETER FRANCIS

"Nope," Bess Marvin said, shaking her head. "Those feathers are wrong. Totally wrong."

"But they're such pretty colors, Bess," eight-year-old Nancy Drew said, holding the plastic bag of feathers in her hand.

"Feathers are feathers," George Fayne insisted.

It was Wednesday afternoon. Nancy and her best friends had gone straight from school to Chippy's Craft Market to buy feathers. But not just any feathers . . .

"Those are hen feathers," Bess said, pointing

to the label on the bag. "We're running in a Turkey Trot tomorrow, not a Hen Heat."

George sighed as she grabbed another bag from the shelf. The feathers in this one were long and white with a brown stripy design. "Totally turkey," she said. "Happy yet?"

Bess read the label on the bag out loud: "'One dozen synthetic turkey feathers.' What does 'syn-thet-ic' mean?"

"I think it means 'fake,'" Nancy said.

"Good enough," George said, tossing the bag into their shopping basket. "Now that we found the right feathers, what do we do with them?"

Reaching into her backpack, Bess pulled out a fashion sketch. "Here's my design for our Turkey Trot costumes," she explained. "All we have to do is glue turkey feathers around the necks of sweatshirts and on leggings. Then we glue a few feathers on our headbands."

Bess ran her hand over the sketch and said, "Simple . . . yet elegant!"

"Simple?" George scoffed. "What's so simple

about gluing hundreds of feathers one by one?"

Nancy liked Bess's design but agreed with George. Gluing so many feathers would take forever. "There's got to be a quicker way," she said.

George's dark curls bounced as she tilted her head in thought. "Here's an idea," she said with a grin. "We squirt sticky maple syrup all over our clothes, dump feathers in front of a fan, turn it on, and—whoosh!"

"I say let's dump that idea, George," Bess said.

Nancy giggled. Bess and George were cousins but as different as turkey and peacock feathers. Bess was a serious fashionista loving the newest styles. George was a tech geek and proud of it. Her style was jeans, sneakers, and definitely not turkey costumes.

"Why do we have to trot in goofy costumes anyway?" George asked as they filled their basket with more turkey feather bags.

"That's the whole idea of the Turkey Trot tomorrow," Nancy explained. "The kid or team with the best turkey costume wins a giant chocolate turkey."

"Not just any chocolate turkey, Nancy," Bess reminded her. "This one is from Classy Coco, the fancy new chocolate store on Main Street."

"I've never tasted Classy Coco's chocolate," Nancy said, "but everyone says it's amazing."

"Just remember our deal, you guys," George said. "If our team wins, we split the chocolate turkey into three pieces—"

"For our Thanksgiving dinners tomorrow," Nancy cut in excitedly. "Go, Galloping Gobblers!"

This wasn't the first time Nancy, Bess, and George teamed up. They also had their own detective club called the Clue Crew. Nancy even had a clue book to write down all their clues and suspects.

"Let's buy the feathers before it gets late," Nancy said. She was about to pick up their basket when—

"Yodel-ay-ee-ooooo . . . Yodel-ay-ee-ooooo!"

The girls froze at the strange sound.

"What was that?" Bess asked.

"It doesn't sound like a turkey gobbling," George said.

"Yodel-ay-ee-ooooo!" There it was again!

Nancy, Bess, and George followed the yodeling to the next aisle. There they saw a girl looking at packaged ribbons.

She was dressed in an embroidered skirt and a puffy-sleeved blouse. Over her blouse was a black velvet vest, and on her blond braided hair was a green felt hat.

To Nancy she looked like a girl from a Swiss storybook. She also looked familiar. . . .

"You guys," Nancy said while the girl kept yodeling. "Isn't that Shelby Metcalf?"

"But Shelby doesn't have long blond hair like me," Bess said. "That girl does."

"Or braids, either," George said.

Shelby turned to the girls and smiled. "It's a wig," she said. "I just need to tie on a few ribbons, and I'm all set!"

"Cool," George said. "But what's with the Heidi costume?"

"Shouldn't you be shopping for a turkey costume?" Nancy asked. "The Turkey Trot is tomorrow on Thanksgiving morning."

"I'm not running in the trot," Shelby said. "I have to get ready for the Pixie Scout International Food Fest on Friday."

"International Food Fest?" Nancy repeated. "You mean there will be food from other countries?"

"Everyone in my troop is bringing a different dish to taste," Shelby explained. "I've been wearing my costume the past few days to get into character.

Shelby opened her mouth to yodel again. To stop her, George quickly cut in. "What food are you bringing, Shelby?" she asked.

"I'm making a Swiss chocolate fondue," Shelby said proudly. "It's where you dip marshmallows, fruit, and pretzels in a pot of melted chocolate. I'm using melted Choco-Wacko bars!"

"Yummy," Bess said. "But too bad the chocolate isn't from Classy Coco."

"You mean that fancy chocolate store on

Main Street?" Shelby asked. "What's so special about that place?"

"My mom is a caterer and told me all about it," George said. "Classy Coco is owned by a woman named Anna Epicure. She used to be the editor of a magazine called *Bon-Bon Vivant*. It's all about chocolate."

"The chocolates in Anna's store are like little statues!" Nancy explained. "I heard she has them made at fancy chocolate factories all over the world!"

"Wow!" Shelby exclaimed. "Forget the Choco-Wacko bars. I'll use Classy Coco chocolate in my fondue!"

"Good luck," George sighed. "One chocolate bar at Classy Coco is the price of fifty Choco-Wacko bars."

"You'd have to sell a lot of lemonade to buy that, Shelby," Bess said. "And it's getting too cold for lemonade."

Shelby's shoulders drooped as she muttered, "Phooey."

"I'm sure your fondue will be great anyway," Nancy said.

"Great isn't enough, Nancy," Shelby said. "My chocolate fondue has to be perfect—no matter what I have to do!"

Shelby tossed a braid over her shoulder and walked away.

"She forgot the ribbons," Bess said. "Ribbons would go great with her costume."

"So would a goat," George joked.

The girls headed straight to the checkout counter. Bess used her Chippy's birthday gift card to buy the turkey feathers.

"Mission accomplished," Bess declared as the girls left the store. "Now let's go home and work on our costumes."

Nancy, Bess, and George walked up Main Street on their way home. Each girl had the same rule: They could walk anywhere as long as it was less than five blocks and as long as they walked together. That was more fun anyway!

"What's that smell?" George asked.

"I didn't use the strawberry shampoo you hate," Bess said, "if that's what you mean."

Nancy noticed the sweet smell too. But it wasn't strawberries. "It's chocolate!" she said excitedly. "I'll bet it's coming from Classy Coco down the block!"

Nancy, Bess, and George neared the store. They could see a reporter and camerawoman from station WRIV-TV standing outside. Also in front of the store was a woman with short dark hair.

"It's Anna Epicure," George whispered. "I saw her picture online."

The girls could hear the reporter ask, "What makes you think you can run a successful chocolate store, Anna?"

"I once ran a successful chocolate magazine, didn't I?" Anna replied. "Running a chocolate store will be a piece of cake."

Anna turned to the camera and quickly added, "Speaking of cake . . . try my Black Forest cake truffles—they're fabulous!"

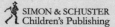